MIA MAYHEM

#6

VS. THE MIGHTY ROBOT

BY **KARA WEST**   ILLUSTRATED BY **LEEZA HERNANDEZ**

LITTLE SIMON

New York London Toronto Sydney New Delhi

LITTLE SIMON
An imprint of Simon & Schuster Children's Publishing Division
1230 Avenue of the Americas, New York, New York 10020
First Little Simon hardcover edition November 2019
Copyright © 2019 by Simon & Schuster, Inc.
Also available in a Little Simon paperback edition
All rights reserved, including the right of reproduction in whole or in part in any form.
LITTLE SIMON is a registered trademark of Simon & Schuster, Inc., and associated colophon is a trademark of Simon & Schuster, Inc.
For information about special discounts for bulk purchases, please contact Simon & Schuster Special Sales at 1-866-506-1949 or business@simonandschuster.com.
The Simon & Schuster Speakers Bureau can bring authors to your live event. For more information or to book an event contact the Simon & Schuster Speakers Bureau at 1-866-248-3049 or visit our website at www.simonspeakers.com.
Designed by Laura Roode
Manufactured in the United States of America 1019 FFG
2 4 6 8 10 9 7 5 3 1
This book has been cataloged with the Library of Congress.
ISBN 978-1-5344-4946-6 (hc)
ISBN 978-1-5344-4945-9 (pbk)
ISBN 978-1-5344-4947-3 (eBook)

CONTENTS

CHAPTER 1

A ROBOT
NAMED JUNIOR

Saturdays are my favorite. Whether it's watching cartoons and movies or playing games, the weekends usually begin at my best friend Eddie's house.

I said hello to his parents, and then I walked into Eddie's room like I have done a hundred times before. This time, though, I was in for the biggest surprise.

There was a robot as tall as me, standing in the middle of the room!

"Oh, hi, Mia!" Eddie cried. "You're right on time. I'm almost done with my latest invention!"

I circled the robot to get a better look. On its front panel, there were big metal letters that spelled "JR."

"Wow! You made a life-size robot!" I said as my jaw dropped to the floor.

My best friend was the smartest person I knew, and he loved all things robots.

"Yup! I named him Junior, and he's going to be my new helper. When I'm done he should be able to help me with, well, everything!"

I leaned in to touch the robot's metal hand. And as soon as my grip tightened, his entire arm snapped off!

"Oh, sorry, Eddie! Sometimes I still can't control my strength," I said with a shrug.

"Don't worry about it. The arm was already loose," he replied.

I gave Eddie a little smile. I knew he was used to my mayhem by now.

You see, the thing is that little accidents like breaking the robot's metal arm aren't strange for me.

Because believe it or not, I'm not just strong—I'm *superhero* strong!

Like for real!

My name is Mia Macarooney, and *I Am. A. Superhero!*

During the day I go to Normal Elementary School, where I'm an ordinary kid, just like Eddie.

But after the school bell rings, I head over to the Program for In Training Superheroes

BRRRING!

aka the PITS. The PITS is a top secret superhero training academy. And at the PITS, I go by Mia Mayhem!

As you can imagine, my weekday schedule is packed. That's why I love Saturday mornings at Eddie's. But today our hangout was going to get cut short. I had to be at the PITS for a special Saturday class.

"Wish you could stay so I could show you more," Eddie said.

I nodded in agreement.

Eddie was my only friend in the whole world who knew my super-secret, and thankfully, he was totally cool with it.

"There are a lot of things Junior can do," Eddie continued. "Like getting you your favorite snack before you go!"

Eddie pushed a button on his remote. Then Junior opened the door, zoomed down the hallway, and turned on his foot blasters to go down the stairs!

ZOOM!

"Hey, Junior, can you grab one of the chocolate-peanut-butter granola bars on the top shelf of the pantry?" Eddie asked when we got to the kitchen.

Junior instantly turned on his laser scanners. Then, when he found the box, he used his powerful hand grippers to bring me a bunch.

I thanked him and then gave Eddie a huge smile. Eddie had invented cool things before, but this new robot was a game changer.

"This is so awesome. Thanks, guys!" I cried, shoving as many bars as I could into my pockets. "See you after class!"

Then I rushed out the door as Eddie and Junior gave me a thumbs-up.

THE MAXIMIZER AND THE MINIMIZER

I sped over to the PITS in record time.
Then I turned the DO NOT ENTER sign that
dangled on the front door.

As soon as I did, a hidden screen
popped up and scanned my face.

The PITS building may look like an
empty warehouse on the outside, but
on the inside it is the coolest place
ever!

Today was my first time going on a Saturday, so I expected the gym to be quiet. But boy, was I wrong! The place was packed with busy superheroes.

Several students were already there practicing different super skills. One boy in a wheelchair was doing a cool flip while the girl next to him was climbing up the ropes. And when I looked up, a few others were doing flying tricks in the air. I didn't see anyone I knew, so I decided to find an open seat on the bleachers.

"Oops, sorry!" I said as I stepped on a kid's toes by mistake.

As soon as he turned around, I knew it was Hugo Fast—the one person I didn't want to see.

"Oh, Mia Mayhem, of course it's you!" he said with a frown.

My cheeks turned bright red.

Hugo and I first met in Dr. Dash's Fast class, where we learned all about superspeed. We had been on a racing team with my friends Penn Powers and Allie Oomph, and let's just say that things hadn't gone smoothly.

I suddenly wished that my friends were with me, but they were in their own training session today with Professor Wingum, the flying professor. I wasn't thrilled to be with Hugo, but I was excited for class to begin.

A professor wearing a bright pink suit and matching hair came bursting through the doors. Her shiny suit had a funky test-tube-and-flask image on it.

"Welcome, class! My name is Dr. Magni Tude, and I'm one of the lead scientists here. Today we'll be learning how to use the newest PITS super-tools!"

She pulled out two small round disks from her pockets. One was blue and other was red.

"These are the Maximizer and the Minimizer, created in our very own PITS Size-o-Metric lab," she explained. "They don't look like much now, but watch this . . ."

With a simple flick of her wrist, she threw the blue disk at a bin of basketballs on the other side of the room.

As soon as the disk hit them, all the balls grew to five times their normal size!

Then just as quickly, the disk flew back into Dr. Tude's hand.

"That was obviously the Maximizer," she said. "Now let's try the Minimizer."

She held the red disk, closed one eye, and took aim. Within seconds the basketballs were back to normal!

Everyone burst into applause as she took a quick bow. Then she pointed to a table covered with disks.

"Today we'll focus on aim and your throwing strength. Those will be the two important skills to master before you are ready to use these tools. Please grab your disks and find the lane that is marked with your name."

Soon I was standing in my lane, holding my own Maximizer and Minimizer, and get this: They had my initials on them!

"Wow, this is cool!" I said with a grin.

I turned around to see if everyone else was as excited as I was. Then I realized I was standing in the lane next to Hugo.

"Hey, Mia! Try not to make too many BIG mistakes," Hugo said with a laugh.

I wasn't going to let him get on my nerves.

So I looked ahead and got ready to throw my first shot.

CHAPTER 3

MISTAKES OF ALL SIZES

But of course first tries never go as planned.

I stood in my lane and waited for the first target to appear. That's when a large platform opened up from the floor and a fluffy pillow came into view.

For this round we had to throw our disks at our pillows to make them giant, which sounds easy enough, right?

Wrong.

I held the blue Maximizer disk up by my face to take aim—but then somehow I dropped it . . . right onto my shoe! I watched in horror as my shoe tripled in size.

I looked around totally embarrassed. Everybody else had successfully hit their pillows, and I knew I had two choices: I could either fix my shoe and fall behind, or I could keep going as if nothing happened.

A too-big shoe couldn't be that much of a problem, right?

Wrong again.

31

I threw the Maximizer toward my target. But somehow, instead of growing large, my pillow disappeared! I looked down at my hands only to find that I had thrown the wrong disk.

And due to my clown-shoe situation, I kept messing up, one throw after another. Sometimes my aim was a little off. Like when I made a baby rattle the size of a car.

Then other times I learned that
some things are just not meant to
be huge (a gigantic slobbery dog is
definitely *not* as cute as you might
think). No matter what I did, I couldn't
seem to get it right.

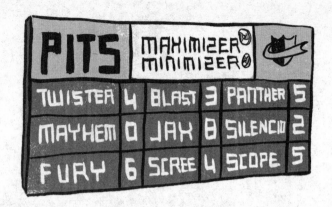

PITS	MAXIMIZER® minimizer®	
TWISTER 4	BLAST 3	PANTHER 5
MAYHEM 0	JAX 8	SILENCIO 2
FURY 6	SCREE 4	SCOPE 5

I looked at the scoreboard that showed how everybody was doing. So far I had gotten zero points.

Next to me, Hugo smirked.

I turned back around to focus on my lane.

Soon, the last item, a toy-size trash can, appeared. We were supposed to make it regular-size, and I had one final chance to do things right.

Of course, just as I was about to throw, Hugo yelled, "Hey, don't miss!" So naturally I almost did.

As soon as I released the disk, I knew
I had definitely thrown it too hard.

The toy-size trash can turned into
a gigantic one, filled with enormous
stinky banana peels. Now, as
if that wasn't bad enough,
instead of coming back to me,

the disk bounced off the floor, knocked back into the trash can, and sent garbage flying everywhere!

I rushed over to the huge, smelly mess. Thanks to my superspeed, I was able to clean up quickly,

and Dr. Tude came over to help. The only problem was that I smelled just as bad as the garbage!

Hugo held his nose as I passed by. "You just can't help living up to your name, can you, Mia MAYHEM?"

I sighed because I knew he wasn't wrong.

CHAPTER 4

THE LOUNGE

Oof. I'd been so excited about Saturday class, and it really couldn't have gone worse. Dragging my heels I headed toward the student lounge. I needed a little pick-me-up before heading back to Eddie's.

When I got to the entrance, a tiny disco light came on as the door swung open.

On the inside there were two different sections.

On the left there was a study section, which had long tables and cool noise-canceling pods if you needed a little peace and quiet.

Then on the right there was a hangout section, which had sofas, a pinball machine, a foosball table, and an entire wall of books and games.

As soon as I walked in, I spotted Penn and Allie on one of the sofas.

They looked like they were both in a great mood, unlike me.

Penn was air drumming, which he did whenever he was really happy. And Allie had removed her metal legs from the bases of her knees so she could rest. Her awesome white kicks had a wing on the side of each shoe that complimented the color of her supersuit.

The two of them waved me over. As I sank into one of the big chairs next to them, I plopped my bag down beside me. And of course I made yet another mess as my stuff spilled out all over the cushion.

Do you ever have days when it feels like nothing goes right? Well, even my bag was having that kind of day. I quickly crammed everything back into my backpack.

HARUMPF!

"Hey, Mia!" cried Allie. "Guess what? We did a flying relay race, and they let me use my rocket blades for the whole class!"

"Yeah, and thanks to Allie, we won first place!" Penn said proudly.

"That's great, you guys," I said with a half-hearted smile.

"How did your training go, Mia?" Allie asked.

I shrugged.

Just thinking about how class had went made my mood go down even more.

"Oh, it was fine," I said. "I'm super-tired though, so I'm going to go home."

My friends nodded as I gave them each a big hug. Then as I walked out the door, I heard Allie ask Penn about a strange, stinky garbage smell.

And that's when I sped away as fast as I could.

I didn't want them to figure out that that stinky smell had been me.

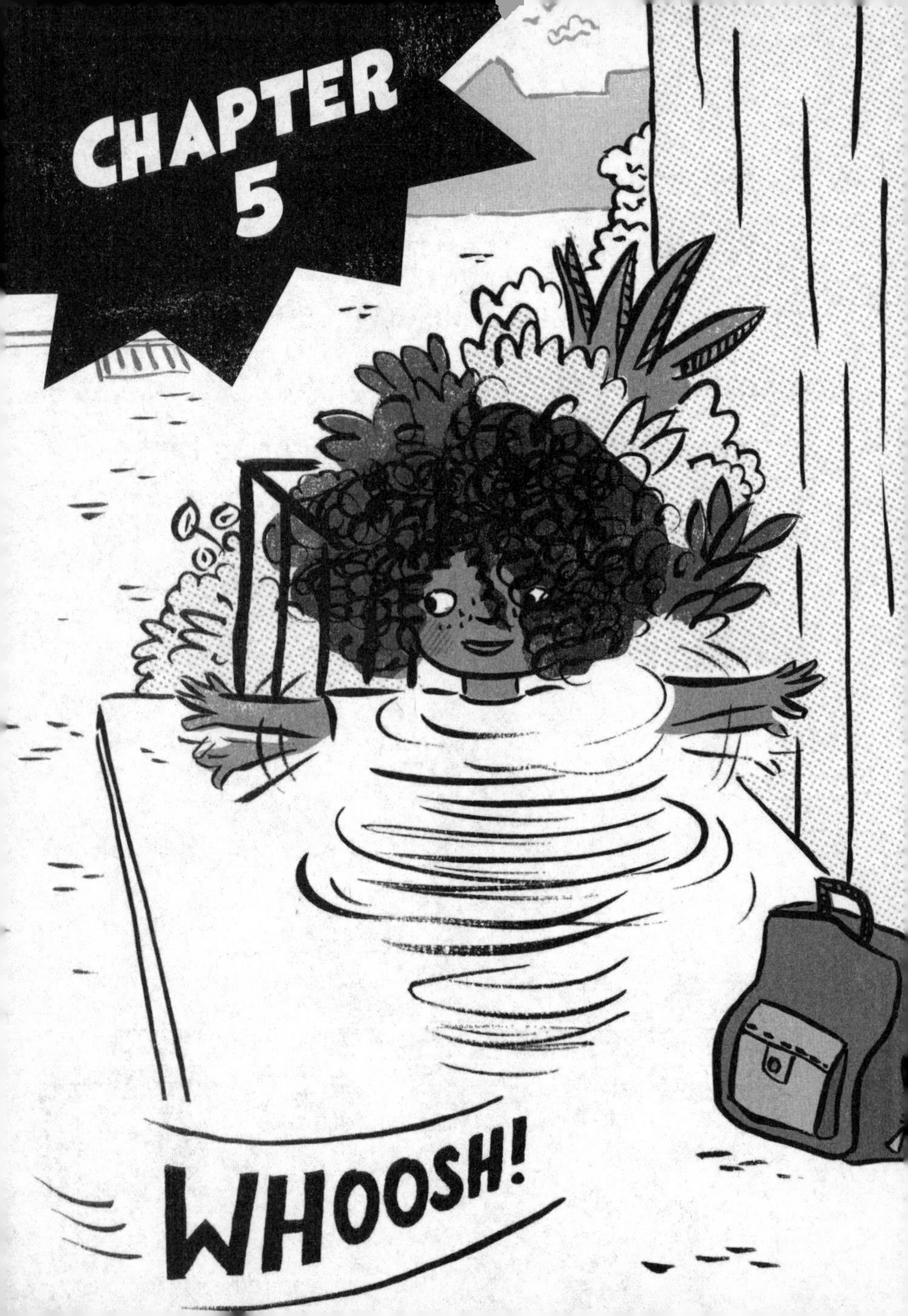
CHAPTER 5
WHOOSH!

Junior Goes Big-Time!

Outside the PITS, I changed back into my regular clothes—thank goodness *they* didn't smell bad.

I decided it was time to go back to Eddie's house. He always knows how to make me feel better when I was having a bad day. I also wanted to see how things were going with Junior, his newest robot helper.

When I got to his house, Eddie was still in exactly the same spot. If I hadn't known better, I'd think he hadn't moved the whole time I was gone.

Eddie was still busy working on the arm that I had pulled off. Junior sat still as the final tweaks were made.

"Looks great!" I said as I plopped into Eddie's beanbag chair. His dog, Pax, was curled up next to it. I scratched his ears as he nuzzled against me.

"Welcome back! How was class?" Eddie asked.

I groaned and told him every single thing that went wrong. I was probably the worst superhero in the history of superheroes.

When I was done he looked at me and said, "Well, you know, at least your shoe is back to normal. And you didn't mess anything up for good. Everything takes time and practice. I mean, look at me! I've been fixing little things in Junior all day! And I build robots *all the time*."

See what I mean? Eddie had the power to always cheer me up.

"Thanks, Eddie!" I said, giving him a smile. "And how about you? Are you almost finished?"

"I think so!" he replied. "He's already been helping me clean up today. Watch!"

He pushed a few buttons on his remote, and there were a few beeps as the lights blinked. In an instant Junior came to life.

CLICK!

BEEP!

He quickly spotted a sock on the floor, walked over to it, picked it up, and tossed it in the laundry hamper.

BEEP - BOP - BEEP - BEEP!

Pretty cool, huh?

But he wasn't done yet.

Junior walked over to my bag, turned it over, and shook it out until every last thing fell out.

Including my smelly supersuit and my new Size-o-Metric disks!

I watched in horror as the Maximizer bounced hard off the floor and slammed directly into Junior . . .

who grew.

And grew.

"Uh-oh," I said as I looked up to the ceiling. "We have a very *big* problem."

CHAPTER
6

THROUGH THE
WINDOW

Everything happened really fast after
that.

Junior had shaken out my bag, and
my stuff was everywhere. I had no clue
where my disks were!

I had to come up with a plan.

And fast.

I grabbed my stinky suit and quick-
changed into Mia Mayhem!

Junior was still growing, and there was only one thing I could do: get him out of the house. If I didn't, he was going to destroy the place from the inside out!

I flew up, picked him up over my head, and was halfway to the window when suddenly we heard a voice in the hallway. It was Eddie's mom!

"Hey, kids?" she called. "Everything okay in there?"

"Um, yeah, Mom!" Eddie called back. "Everything is totally cool and not going wrong in any way! Just doing some of the usual inventing stuff up here!"

"Yes, we're very okay, Mrs. Stein!" I said, trying not to sound like I was holding an expanding robot.

There was a pause and we held our breaths. Then she said, "Okay! Have fun, dears!"

Whew. That was a close one.

Eddie pushed the window open and I flew out just in time. If we were even a second late, Junior would have gotten stuck!

But now what?

I hovered outside of the window as
Eddie checked to make sure his mom
was still downstairs.

All the while, Junior just kept growing. But thanks to my super-strength, it wasn't hard to carry him.

But I had no idea what to do with him. Even at a school like the PITS, they didn't teach you what to do with a giant robot.

"Hey, Eddie!" I called through the window. "I need to get him somewhere away from people."

He nodded in agreement. "Junior's got a tracker on him, so I can follow you on my bike."

Then off I went, carrying Junior through the air.

And here's a little secret, just between you and me: I was a superhero. I could fly, and I had amazing super-strength, and together, I knew Eddie and I would figure things out—even if I didn't know how. But trust me, in *that* moment, I was way more scared than I wanted to admit.

CHAPTER
7

HELP MODE

I flew as fast as I could toward the edge of town.

I flew over the movie theater, the clock tower, and even the park, leaving the center of town far behind. I went farther and farther, until all I could see was the green of treetops.

Finally, I spotted a clearing. This open space would have to do.

As I landed, I placed Junior down carefully and glanced around. It was an old campground! There was a picnic table in the shade and a firepit for roasting s'mores. And more importantly, it was totally empty.

I decided it was time to have a heart-to-heart with Junior. I figured there might be a way to reset his control board. Knowing my best friend, that was the sort of smart thing Eddie probably programmed.

I flew up off the ground, and I'd just gotten up to Junior's eye level when I heard a scream behind me.

I whipped around and discovered three campers, each with backpacks and armloads full of sticks and branches. Two of them were staring in disbelief. One of them was screaming.

So I did the only obvious thing I could think of.

I screamed too.

Turns out the campground wasn't empty after all.

"Um, don't worry! We're not going to hurt you," I started to say when Junior suddenly came to life.

"I AM READY TO HELP!" he yelled in his way-too-loud robot voice.

And then he took two giant steps toward the kids. Before I could stop him, he scooped them all into his hands. The sticks and branches went everywhere!

"I AM CLEANING UP," Junior rumbled.

Oh no.

He was now in cleaning mode, and he thought there was a mess that needed to disappear!

I looked over at Junior's hands—Eddie told me he had installed power grippers this morning. So I 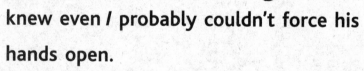 knew even I probably couldn't force his hands open.

But if I couldn't do it myself, maybe I could trick him into releasing the kids!

I grabbed a handful of dirt and looked up at the robot.

"Hey!" I said, throwing the dirt up into the air. "Junior, catch these rocks!"

Junior opened his hand to try to catch the dirt as it fell. That's when I swooped in and caught the kid he was holding.

Success!

Then I did the trick again, and soon, all three kids were safely back on the ground.

"Thank you so much!" they all cheered. "Who are you?"

HOORAY!

"My name is Mia Mayhem," I said as I put on my best serious-superhero face.

"Sorry about that. He wasn't trying to hurt you. But we need to keep this giant robot out of the news. Can I trust you guys not tell anyone that we've met?" I asked, holding my breath.

They all nodded excitedly and then turned around. One of the kids gave me a wink as they walked away.

I let out a sigh of relief. But it was too early to relax.

I turned back to Junior, who was trying to sweep up all the dirt. It was totally *not* working.

"Okay, Junior," I said. "Let's try this heart-to-heart thing again."

But before I could get back up to his eye level, there was a loud

BANG!

CHAPTER 8

BACKUP ARRIVES

I was still trying to figure out what had happened when I saw two figures in supersuits.

As I got closer I realized they were my friends—Penn Powers and Allie Oomph!

"Are you okay, Mia?" called Penn.

"How did you know about Junior?" I asked, totally confused.

"I was standing in line outside the movie theater and spotted something unusual flying overhead," he said. "I decided I needed to check it out."

"And I was in the park," said Allie. "I saw the same thing!"

In an instant I was so relieved. Turns out that being a good superhero really was about being in the right place at the right time.

Because soon Junior started beeping. A lot.

His lights started flashing too.

"Um . . . ," I said. "This is Junior, and I made him really big by mistake."

I had no idea what was going on, but he definitely wasn't in cleaning mode anymore. He started spinning, and as he circled around, he almost hit a group of tall trees! The campers had left a bunch of old branches on the ground, and I watched in a panic as Junior began throwing them.

"What can we do?" Penn asked worriedly. "I tried flying into him when I thought he was attacking you. Maybe I hit a button on his front panel by accident?"

I flew up closer to the robot's chest. And guess what?

That's exactly what happened! Junior was now programmed to throw things out of the way!

All three of us tried to get close to fix him, but it was no use. Junior just kept spinning faster. And at this point whole trees were flying off into the distance.

Junior's voice echoed so loudly over our heads that we had to cover our ears.

Without even discussing it we jumped into action to stop haywire Junior from destroying the whole campground.

With her rocket blades on, Allie was the perfect person to start catching the trees. Every time Junior threw some, she'd fly over, grab the trees, and place them gently onto the ground.

Penn started flying through the forest to collect vines that he could wrap around Junior's legs to bring him down. It was a good plan, except the vines were too flimsy and Junior was too strong!

As for me, I kept trying to get closer to Junior's wiring. I flew in when he stopped to throw things, and tried to hang on while he went spinning. The problem was that every time he stopped, I was way too dizzy!

You'd think three superheroes would be powerful enough for one giant robot, but I'll be honest.

We weren't getting *anywhere*.

CHAPTER
9

THE RIGHT-SIZE SOLUTION

So like I said, things were looking pretty grim.

And that's when I heard a voice call my name. I looked past Junior, toward the trail.

There, on his bike, was Eddie!

"Hey, don't come too close!" I called. "He's gone haywire, and we don't know what he'll do!"

But it was too late. Junior immediately spotted Eddie and stopped spinning. Then he picked Eddie up, and I was afraid Junior was going to throw him like one of those trees!

I quietly motioned Penn and Allie to the ground. Then on the count of three, we each grabbed as much dirt as we could and tossed it into the air.

And thankfully, it worked!

As soon as Junior dropped Eddie, I
swooped in and caught him.

"I'll distract him!" said Penn, flying around Junior's head. "You guys come up with a plan!"

"Okay, don't worry," Eddie said. "I came prepared."

With that, he pulled the remote out of his pocket. He held it out toward Junior and pushed a few buttons.

Nothing.

He pushed a few more buttons.

Still nothing.

"That's weird," he said. "I just changed the batteries!"

Allie landed next to us, sending up a cloud of dust.

"The problem isn't the battery," she said. "It's about the amount of power the battery has! That's a little remote for a little robot. This giant robot"—she pointed over her shoulder to where Junior was trying to catch Penn—"needs a giant remote."

Eddie looked at Allie and nodded. "You're totally right . . . um . . ."

"Oh, I'm Allie Oomph," she said, smiling.

"Eddie Stein, or just Eddie for short," Eddie replied. "Nice to meet you!"

"Guys!" I said, frantically interrupting their meeting. "Where are we going to get a giant remote?"

Eddie reached in his pocket. "How about this?"

It was the Maximizer!

"I couldn't find the other disk, but you could make the remote big with this one, right?"

"Eddie and Allie," I said. "You're both absolute geniuses!"

Eddie set the remote down on the ground. Then I closed one eye and took aim. I really, really hoped I wouldn't miss this time.

And I didn't! It totally worked.

The remote got huge. I finally got it right.

Then Eddie, Penn, and Allie stood on top of the remote as I lifted them into the air.

On the count of three, my friends jumped on the power button. And just like that, Junior finally shut down.

When we were back on the ground, we all gave one another a group high five. We had saved the day as a super-team!

WHEW!

So I wish I could tell you that was the end of the story. We had saved the town from an evil robot takeover!

Well, okay. He wasn't actually an *evil* robot. I guess he was a *nice* robot who went haywire by mistake.

And maybe it wasn't really a *takeover*. I'd say that it was more like total mayhem.

But the good news was that we figured it out together, even if we weren't done quite yet.

We had turned Junior off, but he was still huge! We needed to find the Minimizer—the one that could make Junior small again. So the four of us looked all over Eddie's house. Every single inch. And do you know where we finally found it?

In the doghouse!

Pax had carried it into his bed! It was hidden underneath all his squeaky toys this whole time.

"Pax, this doesn't belong to you," said Eddie, trying to look stern. But Pax just barked and licked Eddie's face while the rest of us tried not to laugh.

After that we took the Minimizer back to the campground and made Junior (and his remote) small again. This time my throws were *perfect*, if I do say so myself!

Then we brought the very *normal-size* robot back to Eddie's house. Today was definitely the most tiring Saturday I've ever had in my life.

But here's another secret: Except for the almost-evil robot stuff—I can't wait for another one like it!

Eddie says he's going to do some very careful rewiring, so Junior can't go haywire anymore, which sounds good to me. And for my part, I'm going to continue doing my target practice with the disks.

But that's all for a later day. For tonight, I'm ready to go back to having a lazy, totally normal weekend with my friends, doing absolutely whatever we want.

121

DON'T MISS
MIA MAYHEM'S
PREVIOUS ADVENTURES!